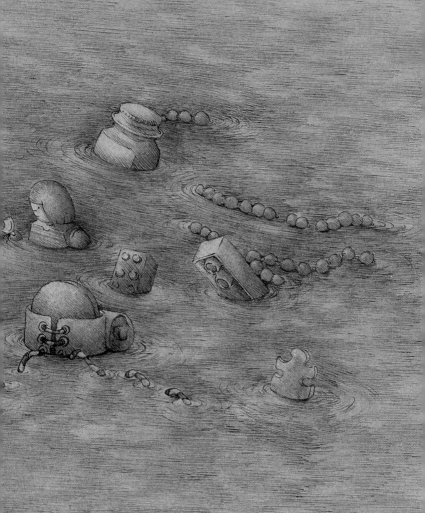

OTHER CREEPIES FOR YOU TO ENJOY ARE:
The Flat Man
Scare Yourself to Sleep
Jumble Joan

For Graham (RI)
For Helen (MK)

School Specialty
Children's Publishing

Text © 1988 Rose Impey
Illustrations © 1988 Moira Kemp
This edition designed by Douglas Martin.

This edition published in the United States of America in 2004 by
Gingham Dog Press
an imprint of School Specialty Children's Publishing,
a member of the School Specialty Family
8720 Orion Place, 2nd Floor, Columbus, OH 43240-2111

www.ChildrensSpecialty.com

Library of Congress Cataloging-in-Publication Data is on file with the publisher

This edition first published in the UK in 2003 by Mathew Price Limited.

ISBN 0-7696-3367-6
Printed in China.

1 2 3 4 5 6 7 8 9 10 MP 08 07 06 05 04

The Ankle Grabber

By Rose Impey
Illustrated by Moira Kemp

GINGHAM DOG
P R E S S

Columbus, Ohio

Every night,
when I go upstairs at bedtime,
I make my mom search through
the whole room.
I do not want to get into bed
until I know that it is safe.

First, Mom draws back the curtains.
She makes sure that
the Flat Man
is not hiding there,
pressed against the glass,
waiting to slide out
and get me when the light goes off.

Next, she looks carefully
through the closet.
She makes sure that Jumble Joan
is not hanging in there,
soft and lumpy,
pretending to be
some old clothes.

Last, she gets down
on her hands and knees.
She searches for
the Ankle Grabber,
who lives in the invisible swamp
underneath my bed.

After Mom checks the room,
she tells me, "It's all clear."
But I can never be quite sure.
I peek around the door and
make a quick dash.
I jump onto my bed
from the middle of the room.

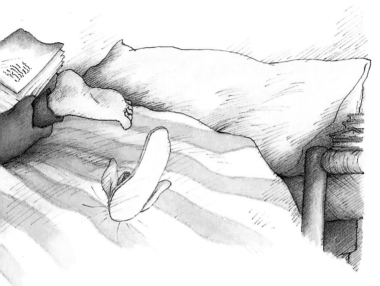

I try to stay far away
from the grabbing hand
underneath my bed.
Its hand may reach up
at any second
and pull me down
by my ankles
into its invisible swamp,
never to be seen again.

I pull the covers
up to my nose
and peek
around the room.

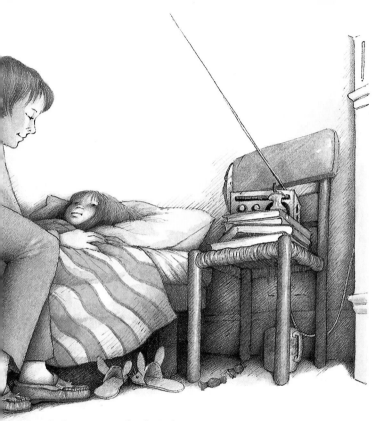

My mom shakes her head.
"I've told you before.
There are no monsters
in this house," she says.
Then, she kisses me goodnight
and goes downstairs.

I lie in bed all alone
in the dark. My head
feels full of monsters.

I think about the Chimney Creeper
and the Guitar Gobbler.
Most of all, I think about
the Ankle Grabber.

I think about
its two beady eyes,
rolling like glass marbles
from side to side
in its hooded head.

They peer out
over the swamp,
looking for anything
that may fall into its grasp.

I think about
its hands,
reaching out with
lizard-like fingers
to get me.

I picture those scaly
fingers slowly creeping
up the side of my bed.

They come closer
and closer until they are
almost touching me.

I shiver
and squeeze myself
into a tight ball
in the middle of my bed.
I tell myself that
if I stay here
without moving,
I will be safe.

The Ankle Grabber cannot get me
because it is stuck
in its slimy swamp.
No matter how much
it stretches
and struggles,
it cannot get out.

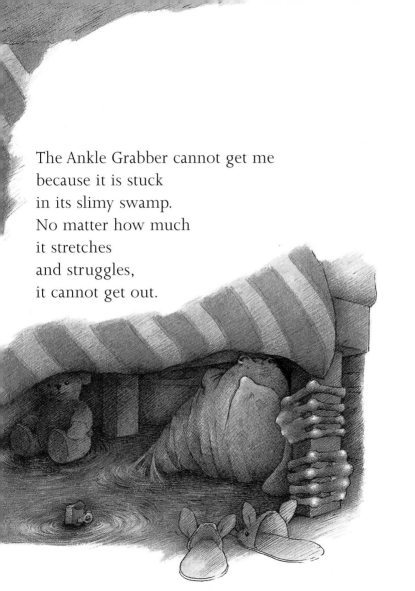

I picture it
sinking back
into the boiling, bubbling mud.

The mud sucks it down
until only two glassy eyes
are left, waiting and watching
in the dark.

I toss and turn,
rolling myself up
in the covers
until I can barely move.
I hate lying here,
wide awake,
with my head full of monsters.

Then, another horrible thought
creeps into my mind.
I need to go to the bathroom.

I tell myself,
I don't need to go to the bathroom,
but I know I do.
I tell myself,
I can wait until the morning,
but I know I can't.

I try to think about something else.
All I can think about is rain,
waterfalls, and dripping faucets.
In the end,
I know I will have to
get out of bed.

I take a deep breath and jump
into the darkness.

I land softly near the door.
I tiptoe along the hallway
and head for the bathroom.

Then, I run back down the hallway.

I take a wild leap
into the room
and fly through the air with
my arms outstreched
like an eagle.

But I miss the bed.
I hit the floor
with a loud bang.

I land facedown on the carpet,
with my head looking
directly under my bed.

I am afraid to look.
I may see
the Ankle Grabber,
watching me.
Any second, his scaly hand
could shoot out and grab me.

Instead, when I look,
I see something else's eyes
staring back at me.
My teddy bear is sitting
on top of the swamp.
I reach out to save him
before he is sucked down
and lost forever.

Suddenly, I stop.

I feel two large hands,
cold and rough,
grabbing my ankles.

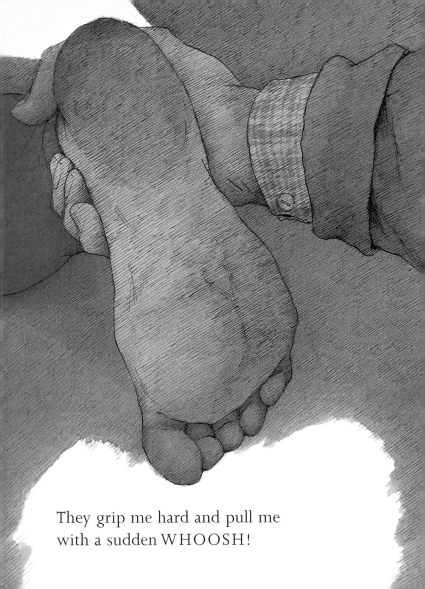

They grip me hard and pull me
with a sudden WHOOSH!

I feel myself sliding
along the bedroom floor.
I start to scream.
"Help! Mom! Dad! Help!"

"What are you doing
   down there?" asks my dad.
I lie on my back and
   look up at him.
I feel pretty silly.
"I thought you were
   the Ankle Grabber," I say.

"So, it's the Ankle Grabber tonight,"
   says Dad, "not the Terrible Toe Twiddler?"
"No," I say, "not him."
"And has the Nasty Knee Nibbler
   been back?" Dad asks.
"No," I say. "You scared him off."

"Then, it sounds like another job
    for the Dreadful Demon Dad.
I will take care of that Ankle Grabber."

"Look out," I call underneath my bed.
"My dad is coming to get you!"